THE STATION MOUSE

MEG MCLAREN

BAGGAGE TAG
PASSENGER
ESCOCIA
00262

PROPERTY OF
THE LOST PROPERTY DEPT.
"IF IT ISN'T LOST WE WON'T FIND IT!"
GUARANTEED

ANDERSEN PRESS LTD
LDN

TRAVEL
BROADENS
THE
RIND

Maurice had been told to stay out of sight.

That was the first rule in the Station Mouse Handbook.
And Maurice liked following the rules.

At night, when the station was empty,
it was Maurice's job to collect
all the things left behind that day.

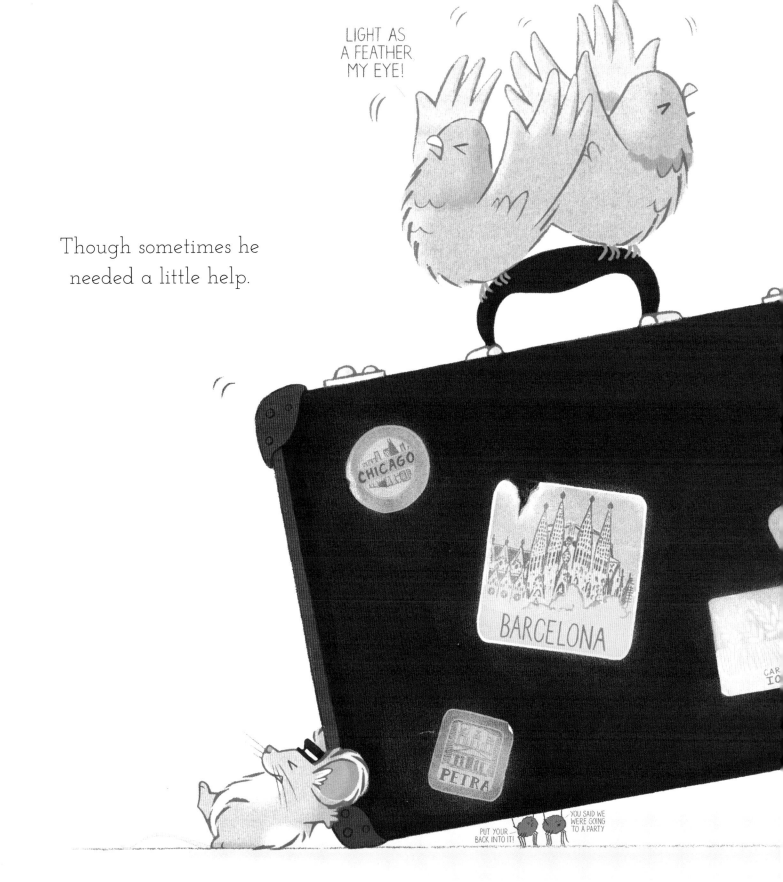

Though sometimes he needed a little help.

Then he slept late into the morning, because of:

RULE 2: A STATION MOUSE MUST
NEVER GO OUT IN THE DAYTIME.

That's when the station is at its busiest.
Passengers, you see, are always rushing
and trains must be caught.

The life of a station mouse
can be a solitary one,

so Maurice liked to
keep himself busy.

AVAST YE
HORNSWAGGLE!

BEACH

Wish
you were
here...

In quieter moments he wondered
why no one came back for
their lost things.

Perhaps the passengers
did not want them
after all?

But what if he was wrong? What if each lost item was
missed and Maurice could do nothing to help?

Because the most
important rule,
the one he must
never break, was:

RULE 3:
A STATION
MOUSE MUST
NEVER
APPROACH THE
PASSENGERS.

Not ever.

Now, there's a reason why these rules exist...

AAARGHHH! MOUSE!

Passengers do not like mice.

Maurice would only be safe if he stayed out of sight.

Mice and passengers don't mix.
That was what the handbook
had taught him.

But, for the very first time,
Maurice knew where a lost thing
belonged and that it **was** wanted, after all.

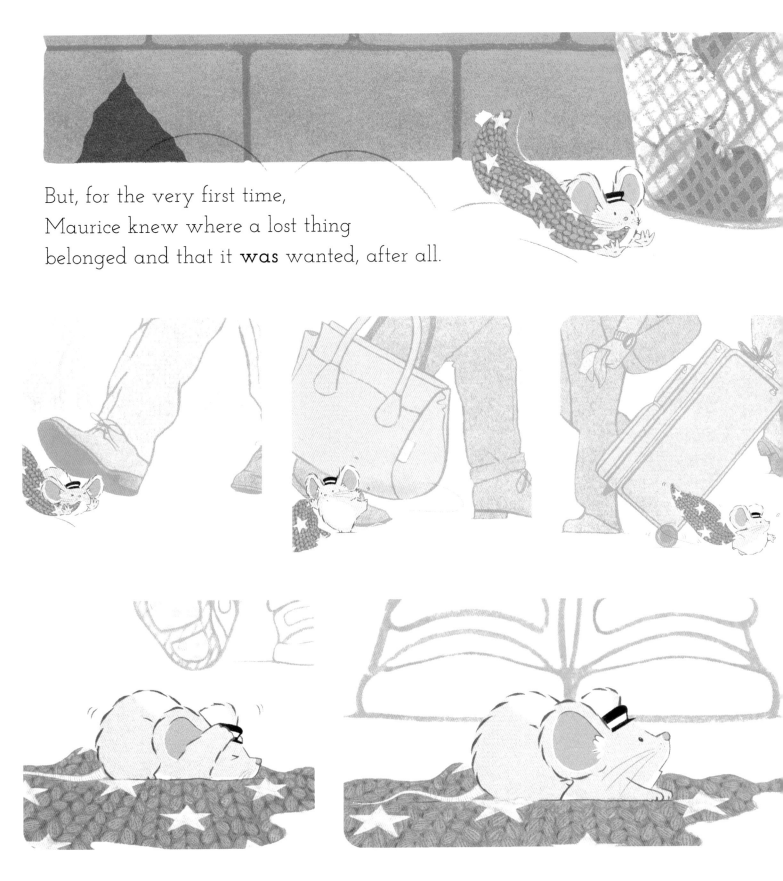

WHICH WAY DID IT GO?

That's when he discovered
that something is only
lost until it is found.

Returning it was
the right thing to do.

Maurice felt better than
he ever had before.

But not for long.

**OOH,
THERE
IT IS!**

**AFTER
IT!**

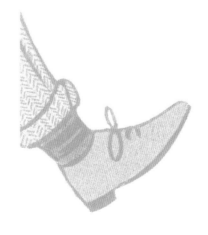

Maurice decided he was going to mind his own business from then on.

The rules were there to protect him.

RIIIINNNG

RIIINNNG

RIIII

THE STATION MOUSE HANDBOOK

Which brings us to the fourth rule:

A station mouse
must never...

hello?

ever...

answer the bell.

Excuse me, I think you dropped your hat.

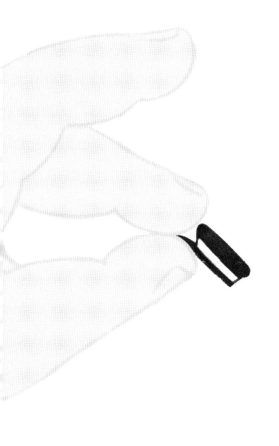

Maurice began to wonder if it was time for a new rule.

Because some passengers **did** like mice. And the rest? Well, they just hadn't got to know him yet.

WAY OUT

RING FOR SERVICE

LEICESTER

RED

LOST PROPERTY

CLO

RING FOR SERVICE

But that was going to change.